BOOK 2 • E♭ Alto Saxophone

COMPREHENSIVE BAND METHOD
by Bruce Pearson

Contributing Editors:
Gerald Anderson & Charles Forque

BEST IN CLASS

Y0-CDQ-346

Dear Student,

Welcome to **BEST IN CLASS, BOOK 2!**

With the skills you are mastering on your instrument, I am sure you are beginning to see how music can add new dimensions to your life.

As you continue to study, you will quickly see that with more proficiency on your instrument comes a greater experience of the beauty and joy of music.

To play your instrument well, careful practice is essential. You will find a chart below to help you keep track of your practice time. Always strive to do your best.

Best wishes in reaching your musical goals!

Bruce Pearson

PRACTICE RECORD CHART

WEEK	DAY 1	DAY 2	DAY 3	DAY 4	DAY 5	DAY 6	DAY 7	TOTAL TIME	PARENT'S INITIALS	WEEKLY GRADE
1										
2										
3										
4										
5										
6										
7										
8										
9										
10										
11										
12										
13										
14										
15										
16										
17										
18										

WEEK	DAY 1	DAY 2	DAY 3	DAY 4	DAY 5	DAY 6	DAY 7	TOTAL TIME	PARENT'S INITIALS	WEEKLY GRADE
19										
20										
21										
22										
23										
24										
25										
26										
27										
28										
29										
30										
31										
32										
33										
34										
35										
36										

© 1983 Kjos West, Publisher, San Diego, California
SBN 0-8497-5878-5   All Rights Reserved   International Copyright Secured   Printed in U.S.A.

DAILY WARM-UPS . . . for alto saxophones only

A. STEADY TONE

★ Always play with your best tone. Keep your tone steady.
   1. Play each note $p \!=\!\!=\! f \!=\!\!=\! p$
   2. Play each note with the following articulation pattern: ♩ ♩ ♪♪♪♪ . Strive for a clean attack on each note.

B. SMOOTH SLURS

★ Keep your embouchure steady for all notes.

C. SCALE STUDY

1st time — slur   2nd time — tongue lightly

D. ARTICULATION ANTICS

★ Strive for a clean attack on all tongued notes.

E. INTERVAL STRETCH

★ Can you play this in one breath?

1. MOVING CHORDS

Band Arrangement

2. TECHNIC TRAINER

3. G MAJOR (B♭ Concert) SCALE, THIRDS, AND ARPEGGIOS

★ Write in the note names before you play.

THEORY
GAME

W4XE

4

| ACCENT | | Play the note with the accent (>) a little louder. |

11. LITTLE BROWN JUG
Joe Winner

| EIGHTH REST | ɣ = 1/2 beat of silence
An eighth rest is half as long as a quarter rest. | 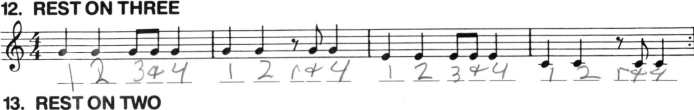 |

1. Before you play exercises 12 through 16, write in the counting.   2. Then clap and count the rhythm.

12. REST ON THREE

13. REST ON TWO
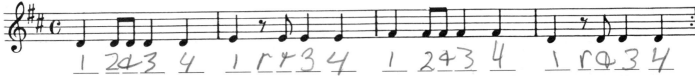

14. REST ON FOUR

15. REST OFF THE BEAT

16. REST ON THE BEAT

17. THE GOOD KING HAS RHYTHM

SOMETHING SPECIAL . . . for alto saxophones only

★Move your fingers quickly and use a continuous air stream.

SPECIAL EXERCISE

W4XE

NEW IDEA

| SYNCOPATION |  | Play an accent on a note that is normally not a strong pulse. |

18. PLAY IT STRONG

★ Write in the counting before you play.

19. SHOO-FLY

Moderato

Frank Campbell

mf

20. NOBODY KNOWS THE TROUBLE I'VE SEEN

Andante

Spiritual

mp

21. LIZA JANE

Allegro

Afro-American Folk Song

22. A LATIN LUNCH

Moderato

Root/Pearson — Band Arrangement

1st time - *mf*   2nd time - *f*

NEW IDEA

| LONG REST |  | Rest for the number of measures that are indicated. |

23. HOW LONG IS YOUR REST?

Count: 1, 2 — 2, 2

SOMETHING SPECIAL . . . for alto saxophones only

Moderato

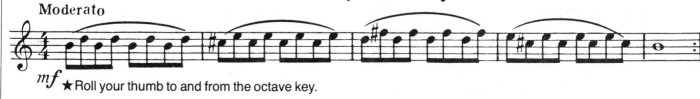

mf ★ Roll your thumb to and from the octave key.

SPECIAL EXERCISE

W4XE

NEW IDEA

| ONE MEASURE REPEAT | | Repeat the previous measure. |

24. THE TENDERFOOT POLKA

Root/Pearson — Band Arrangement

★ Write in the counting before you play.

NEW IDEA

| KEY SIGNATURE |  Key Name: F Major (A♭ Concert) | When you see this key signature, play all B's as B flats. |

THEORY GAME

25. F MAJOR (A♭ Concert) SCALE AND ARPEGGIOS

★ Circle the notes changed by the key signature before you play.

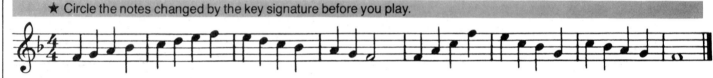

NEW NOTES

26. SIMILAR SOUNDS

★ These two notes are enharmonic.   1st time — play the upper notes   2nd time — play the lower notes

27. OLD JOE CLARK

Tennessee Folk Song

NEW NOTE

28. CHROMATIC CAPERS

29. ENHARMONIC HOP

W4XE

SPECIAL
EXERCISES

NEW
IDEAS

THEORY
GAME

SOMETHING SPECIAL . . . for alto saxophones only

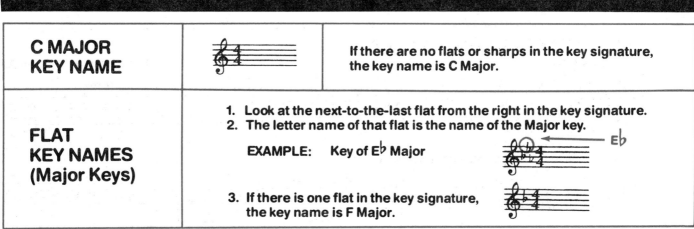

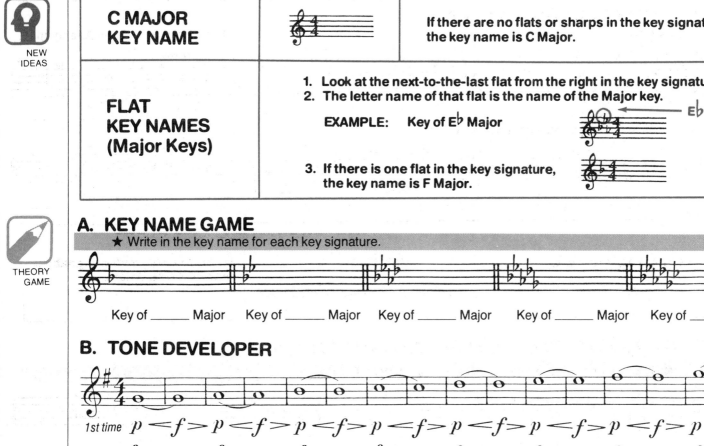

A. KEY NAME GAME

★ Write in the key name for each key signature.

Key of _____ Major   Key of _____ Major   Key of _____ Major   Key of _____ Major   Key of _____ Major

B. TONE DEVELOPER

1st time $p < f > p < f > p < f > p < f > p < f > p < f > p < f > p < f$

2nd time $f > p < f > p < f > p < f > p < f > p < f > p < f > p < f > p$

C. C MAJOR (E♭ Concert) SCALE, THIRDS, AND ARPEGGIOS

1st time - play the lower notes   2nd time - play the upper notes

D. TECHNIC TRAINER

E. ALTERNATE FINGERINGS

★Use the chromatic F♯ fingering.

★Use the chromatic C fingering.

W4XE

30. KEY SIGNATURE CRAZE

★ Circle the notes changed by each key signature before you play.

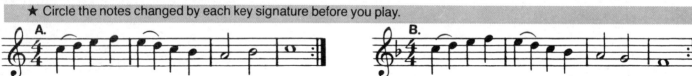

31. SONATINA

Ludwig van Beethoven

★ What is the key name for **SONATINA?** _____

NEW IDEA

TIME SIGNATURE	¢ = 2 beats in each measure (ALLA BREVE or CUT TIME)	o = 2 beats = d = 1 beat = ♪ = 1/2 beat = ‡	¢

32. CUT TIME

★ Write in the counting before you play.

33. OATS AND BEANS

American Folk Song

34. OH, SUSANNA

Stephen Foster

★ Write in the counting before you play.

35. STARS AND STRIPES FOREVER

John Philip Sousa

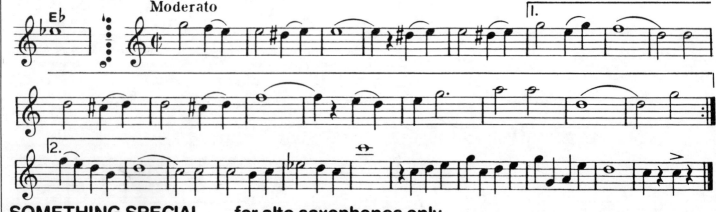

SOMETHING SPECIAL . . . for alto saxophones only

NEW NOTES

★ These two notes are enharmonic.   ★ Be sure to roll your finger from D♯ or E♭ to C.

THEORY GAME

36. MARK TIME MARCH

Root/Pearson — Band Arrangement

★ What is the key name for **MARK TIME MARCH?** ____________________

Moderato

NEW IDEAS

STACCATO		Play the notes separated. Play the notes for half of their original value.	
LEGATO		Play the notes as smoothly and as connected as possible. Use a "du" syllable.	

37. STACCATO AND LEGATO

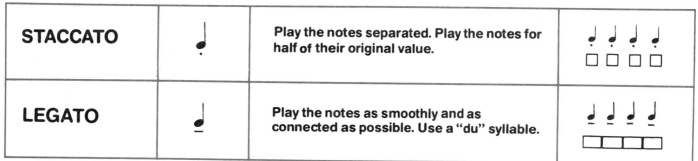

★ Separate the staccato notes and sustain the legato notes.

38. THEME FROM "SURPRISE SYMPHONY"

Andante

Franz Joseph Haydn

NEW IDEA

SIMILE	*simile* (*sim.*)	**Continue in the same way.**

39. TECHNIC TRAINER

Moderato

★ How's your wind speed?

SPECIAL EXERCISE

SOMETHING SPECIAL . . . for alto saxophones only

Moderato

NEW IDEA

D.S. AL FINE	D. S. (del segno) = sign Fine = finish	When you see the *D. S. al Fine*, go back to the 𝄋 (sign) and stop when you come to the *Fine*.

40. THE ASH GROVE

Moderato

Old Welsh Air

41. CRIPPLE CREEK

Traditional

★ Write in the note names before you play.

Allegro

mf

42. TECHNIC TRAINER

Allegro

mf

★Constant air and quick fingers will make this easier!

43. LITTLE DANCE

Franz Joseph Haydn

Moderato

★ Write in the counting before you play.

SOMETHING SPECIAL . . . for alto saxophones only

c♯/D♭

Moderato

f

★Tongue lightly.

★ These two notes are enharmonic.

THEORY GAME

SPECIAL EXERCISE

NEW NOTES

44. THE HIGH SCHOOL CADETS MARCH

Allegro

John Philip Sousa

45. MARACAS GO UP AND DOWN

Allegro

Mexican Folk Song

★ Keep your fingers close to the keys.

SIXTEENTH NOTE

♬ = 1/4 beat

A sixteenth note is half as long as an eighth note.

46. RHYTHM MIX

Moderato

★ Write in the counting before you play.

47. OLD BRASS WAGON

Moderato

Southern Tune

48. JING-A-LING

American Camp Song

49. STEADY AS YOU GO

★ What is the key name for **STEADY AS YOU GO?** _____

1st time — play the upper notes   2nd time — play the lower notes

50. TECHNIC TRAINER

SOMETHING SPECIAL . . . for alto saxophones only

Andante

NEW IDEA

THEORY GAME

SPECIAL EXERCISE

NEW NOTE

W4XE

51. SOURWOOD MOUNTAIN

Moderato

American Folk Song

mf

EIGHTH AND SIXTEENTH NOTE COMBINATIONS

52. GRASSHOPPERS' GIG

★ Write in the counting before you play.   *1st time — play the upper notes*   *2nd time — play the lower notes*

53. HOPPER-GRASS HOP

★ Write in the counting before you play.

54. EZEKIEL SAW THE WHEEL

Moderato

Spiritual

mp

mf

mp

KEY SIGNATURE

Key Name: **A Major (C Concert)**

When you see this key signature, play all F's as F sharps, all C's as C sharps, and all G's as G sharps.

55. A MAJOR (C Concert) SCALE

★ Circle the notes changed by the key signature before you play.

56. CHROMATIC SCALE

chromatic

enharmonic

SOMETHING SPECIAL . . . for alto saxophones only

chromatic

NEW IDEA

NEW NOTES

THEORY GAME

NEW NOTES

SPECIAL EXERCISE

NEW NOTE

W4XE

SOMETHING SPECIAL . . . for alto saxophones only

SPECIAL
EXERCISES

NEW IDEA

**SHARP
KEY NAMES
(Major Keys)**

1. Look at the last sharp to the right in the key signature.
2. The letter name of the next line or space above is the name of the Major key.

    EXAMPLE: Key of D Major

3. If there are six sharps in the key signature, the key name is F♯ Major.

4. If there are seven sharps in the key signature, the key name is C♯ Major.

A. KEY NAME GAME

THEORY
GAME

★ Write in the key name for each key signature.

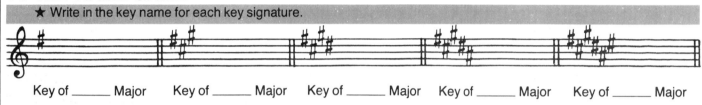

Key of _____ Major   Key of _____ Major   Key of _____ Major   Key of _____ Major   Key of _____ Major

B. F MAJOR (A♭ Concert) SCALE, THIRDS, AND ARPEGGIOS

C. ALTERNATE FINGERINGS

NEW
NOTES

D. CHROMATIC SCALE

NEW NOTE

★ Use chromatic fingerings.

W4XE

57. MARIANNI
Italian Folk Song

★ What is the form of **MARIANNI?** _____

58. MOVIN' ON UP

59. THE RIDDLE SONG
American Folk Song

60. TECHNIC TRAINER

★ What is the key name for **TECHNIC TRAINER?** _____

61. IRISH JIG
Irish Folk Song

1st time — play the lower notes   2nd time — play the upper notes

62. MUSETTE
Johann Sebastian Bach

1st time — play the upper notes   2nd time — play the lower notes

63. CAN YOU GUESS MY NAME?

★ Write in the counting before you play.

SOMETHING SPECIAL . . . for alto saxophones only

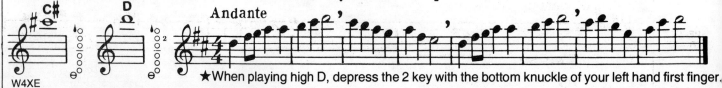

Andante

★ When playing high D, depress the 2 key with the bottom knuckle of your left hand first finger.

W4XE

64. ARTICULATION ANTICS

NEW IDEA

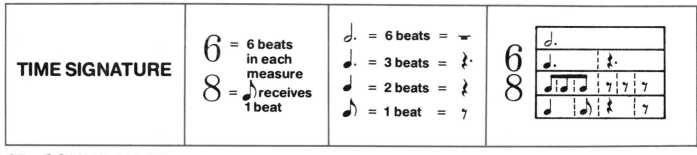

65. COUNT ON IT

1st time — play the upper notes   2nd time — play the lower notes

1. Count out loud and write in the counting before you play.   2. Clap the rhythm before you play.

66. THE BEAT GOES ON

★Did you feel 6 beats in each ♩. ?

67. THREE IN ONE

★Feel 3 beats in each ♩. .

68. TWO IS BETTER THAN ONE

★ Be sure to give the ♩ 2 beats.

69. OFF AND ON

70. FIDDLE-DEE-DEE

English Folk Song

SOMETHING SPECIAL . . . for alto saxophones only

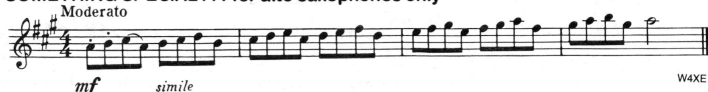

SPECIAL EXERCISE

W4XE

NEW IDEA

TIME SIGNATURE	$\begin{array}{l}3 \\ 8\end{array}$ = 3 beats in each measure / ♪ receives 1 beat	♩. = 3 beats = 𝄼. / ♩ = 2 beats = 𝄼 / ♪ = 1 beat = 𝄿	

71. DUET FOR HAND CLAPPERS AND KNEE SLAPPERS

Hand Clappers

Knee Slappers

72. TECHNIC TRAINER

★ Write in the counting and clap the rhythm before you play.

NEW IDEA

D.S. AL CODA	*D. S. (del segno)* = **sign** *al Coda* = **to Coda**	When you see the *D. S. al Coda* go back to the 𝄋 (sign). When you come to the ⊕ (Coda sign), skip to the Coda.

73. BACK TO THE 50'S

Moderato

Root/Pearson — Band Arrangement

to Coda ⊕

⊕ Coda

D. S. al Coda

SPECIAL EXERCISE

SOMETHING SPECIAL . . . for alto saxophones only

NEW NOTES

W4XE

1st time — play the lower notes   *2nd time — play the upper notes*

74. TECHNIC TRAINER

★ Be sure to keep your fingers close to the keys.

75. EIGHTH NOTES AND RESTS

A.

B.

C.

D.

E.

76. GERMAN DANCE

Franz Joseph Haydn

★ What is the key name for **GERMAN DANCE**? _____

Moderato

mp

THEORY
GAME

77. VIVE LA COMPAGNIE

French Folk Song

Solo/Soli

mp

div. **Tutti**

mf

Solo/Soli

mp

div. **Tutti**

f

Solo/Soli

div. **Tutti**

SOMETHING SPECIAL . . . for alto saxophones only

Moderato

f

★ Tongue very lightly.

SPECIAL
EXERCISE

W4XE

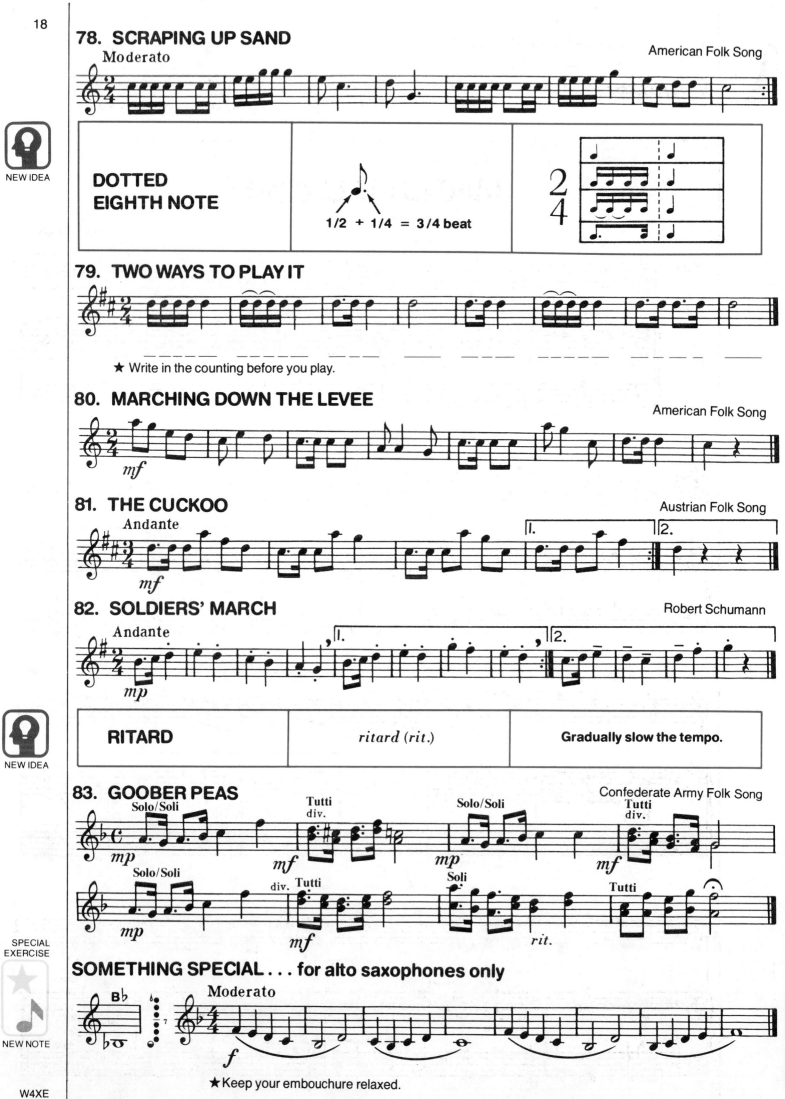

78. SCRAPING UP SAND

Moderato

American Folk Song

DOTTED EIGHTH NOTE	1/2 + 1/4 = 3/4 beat	2/4

79. TWO WAYS TO PLAY IT

★ Write in the counting before you play.

80. MARCHING DOWN THE LEVEE

American Folk Song

mf

81. THE CUCKOO

Austrian Folk Song

Andante

mf

82. SOLDIERS' MARCH

Robert Schumann

Andante

mp

RITARD	*ritard (rit.)*	Gradually slow the tempo.

83. GOOBER PEAS

Confederate Army Folk Song

Solo/Soli   *mp*   Tutti div.   *mf*   Solo/Soli   *mp*   Tutti div.   *mf*

Solo/Soli   *mp*   div. Tutti   *mf*   Soli   Tutti   *rit.*

SOMETHING SPECIAL . . . for alto saxophones only

Moderato

f

★ Keep your embouchure relaxed.

W4XE

NEW IDEA

DYNAMICS	ff = *fortissimo* pp = *pianissimo*	Play with a very loud volume. Play with a very soft volume.

MAGIC MOUNTAIN

W4XE

84. THE HUNTING HORN

4-Part Round

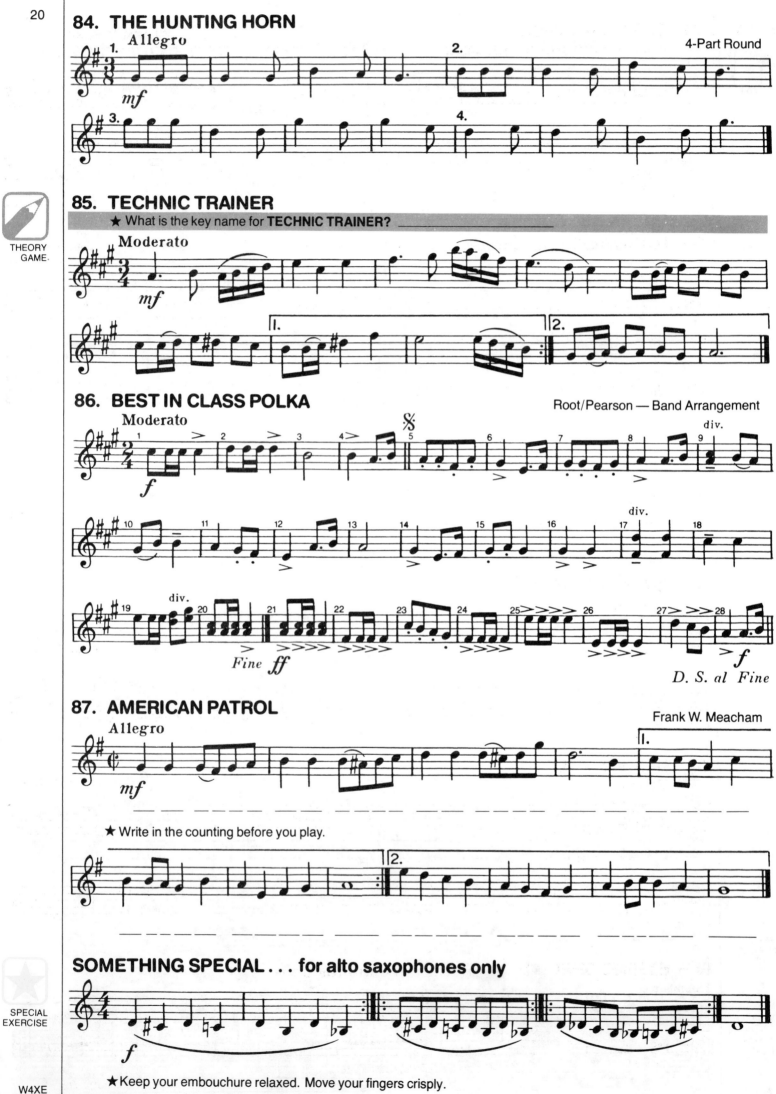

85. TECHNIC TRAINER

★ What is the key name for **TECHNIC TRAINER?** _____

86. BEST IN CLASS POLKA

Root/Pearson — Band Arrangement

87. AMERICAN PATROL

Frank W. Meacham

★ Write in the counting before you play.

SOMETHING SPECIAL . . . for alto saxophones only

★ Keep your embouchure relaxed. Move your fingers crisply.

THEORY GAME.

SPECIAL EXERCISE

THEORY
GAME

88. CONTRA-DANSE
Wolfgang Amadeus Mozart

★ What is the form of **CONTRA-DANSE?** _____

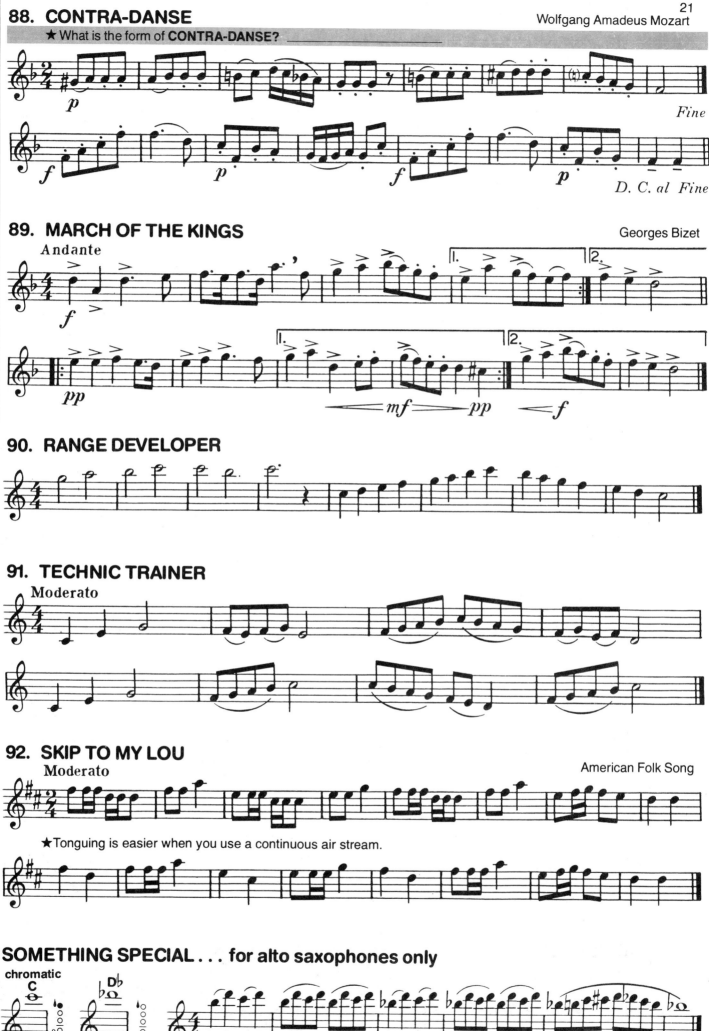

Fine

D. C. al Fine

89. MARCH OF THE KINGS
Georges Bizet

Andante

90. RANGE DEVELOPER

91. TECHNIC TRAINER
Moderato

92. SKIP TO MY LOU
Moderato
American Folk Song

★ Tonguing is easier when you use a continuous air stream.

SPECIAL
EXERCISE

NEW
NOTES

SOMETHING SPECIAL . . . for alto saxophones only

chromatic

★ Use the chromatic C fingering.

enharmonic

W4XE

NEW NOTE

93. EL CAPITAN MARCH

John Philip Sousa

Allegro

94. CAN YOU COUNT IT?

Moderato

★ Write in the counting before you play.

NEW IDEA

| KEY SIGNATURE |  Key Name: B♭ Major (D♭ Concert) | When you see this key signature, play all B's as B flats and all E's as E flats. |

THEORY GAME

95. B♭ MAJOR (D♭ Concert) SCALE, THIRDS, AND ARPEGGIOS

★ Circle the notes that are changed by the key signature before you play.

★ Use the alternate B♭ fingering.

96. ALOUETTE

French Traditional Song

Tutti   Solo/Soli   Tutti

Solo/Soli   Tutti   Solo/Soli   Tutti   Solo/Soli   Tutti

SPECIAL EXERCISE

NEW NOTES
W4XE

SOMETHING SPECIAL . . . for alto saxophones only

E♭/D#

Moderato

★ When playing high E♭/D#, add the 1 key using the middle knuckle of your left hand first finger.

★ These two notes are enharmonic.

SPECIAL
EXERCISES

SOMETHING SPECIAL . . . for alto saxophones only

A. PHRASES, PHRASES

Andante

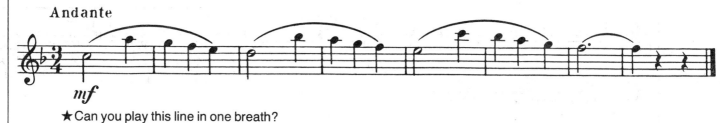

★ Can you play this line in one breath?

B. D MAJOR (F Concert) SCALE, THIRDS, AND ARPEGGIOS

1st time — slur   2nd time — play legato

C. TECHNIC TRAINER

D. TONGUING TRAINER

★ Continue the same rhythm pattern on the following notes:

E. CHROMATIC SCALE

★ Remember to use the chromatic fingerings.   *1st time — slur   2nd time — play legato*

W4XE

THEORY GAME

NEW IDEA

97. DOWN BY THE STATION

2-Part Round

★ What is the key name for **DOWN BY THE STATION?** _____

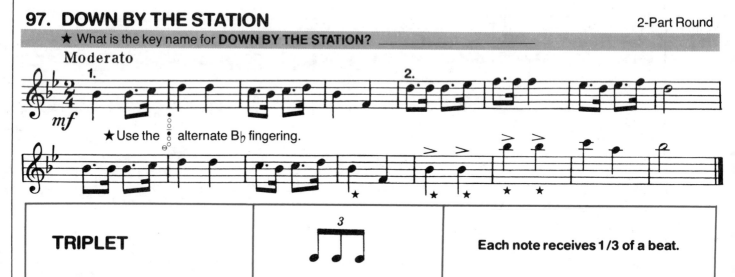

★ Use the alternate B♭ fingering.

TRIPLET		Each note receives 1/3 of a beat.

98. TRIPLETS, TRIPLETS, AND MORE TRIPLETS

★ Write in the counting before you play.

99. PILGRIMS' CHORUS

Richard Wagner

100. CHROMATIC CAPERS

★ Play this exercise again using each of the following articulations:

SOMETHING SPECIAL . . . for alto saxophones only

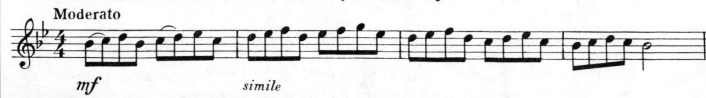

SPECIAL EXERCISE

101. ROLLIN' ROCK

Root/Pearson — Band Arrangement

102. TECHNIC TRAINER

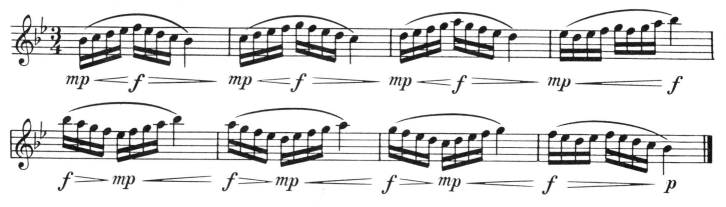

103. OUT FOR THE COUNT

★ Write in the counting before you play.

SOMETHING SPECIAL . . . for alto saxophones only

W4XE

★ Use the alternate fingering for all B♭'s.

104. CAN-CAN

Jacques Offenbach

105. TONGUING TRAINER

★ Write in the counting before you play.

106. MARCH FROM "NUTCRACKER SUITE"

Peter Ilyich Tchaikovsky

107. TECHNIC TRAINER

SPECIAL
EXERCISE

NEW
NOTES

SOMETHING SPECIAL . . . for alto saxophones only

★When playing high F, add the 3 key using the first knuckle of your left hand second finger

108. CHROMATIC SCALE

★ Memorize this scale. *1st time — play the upper notes   2nd time — play the lower notes*

109. ARKANSAS TRAVELER

Moderato

Folk Song

mf

opt.

opt.

110. FATHER OF VICTORY

L. Ganne

f ★Are you playing with a constant air stream and a good hand position?

111. CAN YOU COUNT IT?

Fine

★ Write in the counting before you play.

D.C. al Fine

NEW IDEA

SIXTEENTH REST	𝄿 = 1/4 beat of silence **A sixteenth rest is half as long as an eighth rest.**	2/4

THEORY GAME

112. SIXTEENTH STUDY

1. On each of the following exercises, write in the counting before you play. 2. Play each exercise 4 times.

A.

B.

C.

D.

113. THE GLENDY BURK

Stephen Foster

★ Write in the counting before you play.

114. RULE BRITANNIA

English Folk Song

115. THEME FROM "SWAN LAKE"

Peter Ilyich Tchaikovsky

★ Write in a breath mark at the end of each phrase.

D.C. al Fine

116. TECHNIC TRAINER

★ What is the key name for **TECHNIC TRAINER?** _____

THEORY GAME

SOMETHING SPECIAL . . . for alto saxophones only

SPECIAL EXERCISE

★ Keep your embouchure relaxed for the lower notes.

W4XE

SOMETHING SPECIAL . . . for alto saxophones only

A. GOING UP?

★ Can you play this line in one breath?

B. A MAJOR (C Concert) SCALE, THIRDS, AND ARPEGGIOS

1st time — slur   2nd time — play legato

C. TECHNIC TRAINER

★ Slide your right little finger firmly when playing E♭ to C or C to E♭.

D. BROKEN CHORDS

E. TONGUING TRAINER

★ Continue the same rhythm pattern on the following notes:

F. CHROMATIC SCALE

1st time — slur   2nd time — play legato

W4XE

117. MARCH FROM "AIDA"

Giuseppe Verdi

118. OUR DIRECTOR MARCH

F.E. Bigelow

119. BATTLE HYMN OF THE REPUBLIC

William Steffe

★ What is the key name for **BATTLE HYMN OF THE REPUBLIC?** _____

120. MARCH FOR DEE

Root/Pearson — Band Arrangement

W4XE

SCALE STUDIES

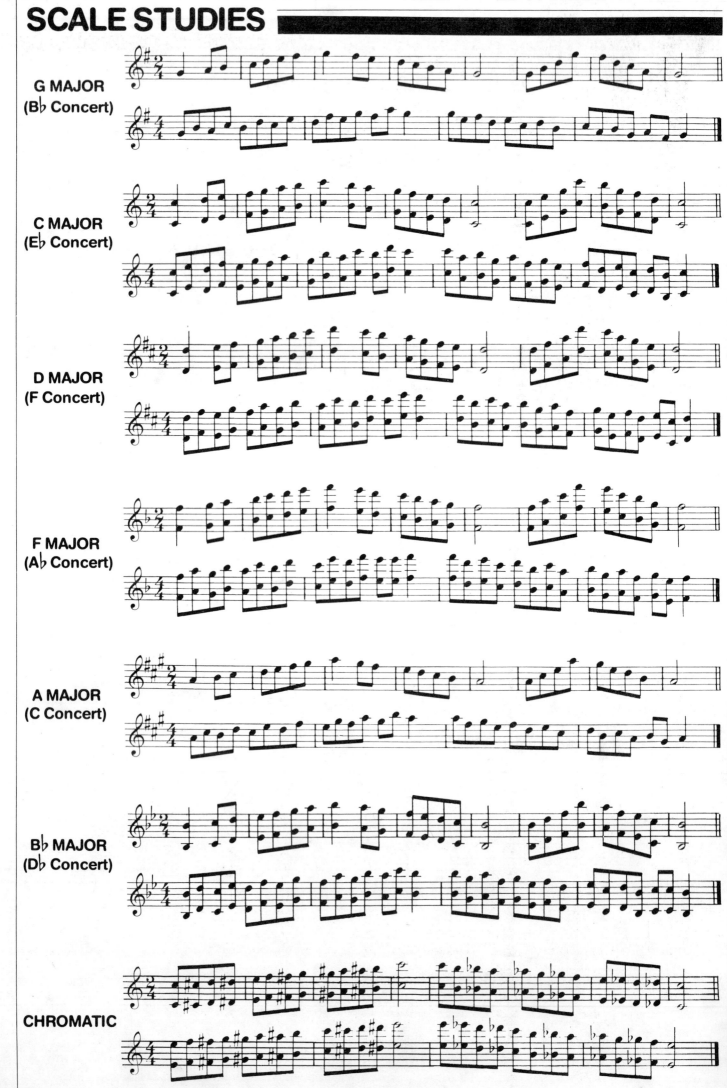

G MAJOR
(B♭ Concert)

C MAJOR
(E♭ Concert)

D MAJOR
(F Concert)

F MAJOR
(A♭ Concert)

A MAJOR
(C Concert)

B♭ MAJOR
(D♭ Concert)

CHROMATIC